The Enchanted Anklet

A CINDERELLA STORY
FROM INDIA

translated & adapted

by

Lila Mehta

illustrated by

Neela Chhaniara

Lilmur Publishing

The Enchanted Anklet

ISBN: 0-9692729-0-1

To:

Murray Horowitz

Without whose encouragement and assistance

this book would not have become a reality.

The author wishes to thank

Alyson McLelland

Trevor Ludski

Les Parsons

of the Scarborough Board of Education

for their help and inspiration

&

Navin Mehta

for moral support and assistance

with front book cover design.

Foreword

Each language, culture and ethnic tradition displays its distinctive style and values in the peculiar tales it devises and in its reworking of common tales shared by many peoples. The typical "Cinderella" tale — an abused, unwanted girl gains the favor of a wonder-working benefactor and thereby escapes all obstacles, meets, loses and finally reunites with her Prince Charming through a surprising means of identification — is found in many lands in many forms. To these is now added a sprightly Indo-Canadian version from the pen of Lila Mehta, teacher by profession and avid student and exponent of things cultural, especially myth and folklore.

In this version, the timeless themes are still to be found, but strikingly presented in the East Indian fashion of saris, golden anklets and festival of the goddess, not gowns, glass slippers and feudal ball. Yet more striking is Godfather Snake with his magic jewel, appearing in the role some of us have come to equate with Fairy Godmother with her magic wand. In the culture of India, as in the myth, religion and folklore of many traditional cultures, the snake is an ancient and complex symbol: sometimes male, sometimes female; maybe vicious, maybe benign; an ambivalent figure of no fixed shape, but possessed of power and uncanny sense. To unfortunate humans of no power or status of their own, the snake may symbolize not only danger, but (as Godmother or Godfather!) one's last best hope in a strange and hostile world. The fabled jewel on the viper's head has long since been a favorite motif of Indian myth and folklore: the magic stone granting all one's wishes — if only one dare reach for it, and the snake be kind enough to let it go.

The "Cinduri-Cinderella" tale, rooted as it is in common human experiences of deprivation and hope and articulated in parallel versions of a common plot, demonstrates that communication between cultural traditions need not be difficult and irksome, at least not by the route of folklore and fairy tale. We are therefore fortunate in having with us in Toronto practitioners of these folk arts: tellers of tales and painters of pictures like Lila and Neela. They stimulate our imagination and take us further along the road of establishing a coherent multicultural society in Canada.

Joseph T. O'Connell, Professor
St. Michael's College, University of Toronto
Toronto, Ontario, Canada
October 21, 1986

Cinduri had to carry
heavy pots of water.

Far away and long ago, before the *Vikram** dynasty, there lived in India a farmer named Cindur in a little town called Cindurnagar. It was customary in those days for an East Indian to have more than one wife. Cindur had married two ladies to help him with the farm. Each wife in turn bore a baby daughter. The first wife's daughter was named Cinduri, and the daughter of the second wife was named Lata. Cinduri's mother died during a cholera epidemic; a few days later, her father became ill and died also.

Cinduri was left to depend on her stepmother who provided a home for her. She grew up to be a beautiful girl, with skin as smooth as silk, exquisite almond eyes, and lips tinged like a pomegranate. Her stepmother was very jealous of Cinduri's beauty, for her own daughter, Lata, was plain and ugly. Accordingly, she gave poor Cinduri all the menial, unpleasant and the heaviest tasks.

Every day, Cinduri had to walk a long way with heavy pots on her head to fetch the drinking water from the lake. She had to cook, clean the house, milk, tend the cows and buffaloes, churn the butter, and then go from house to house to sell vegetables, milk and butter. She was given drab and tattered rags to wear and had to walk barefoot through mud and dirt roads. She was never allowed to go to the city. Her stepmother and Lata went everyday to the city in a horse drawn carriage. They ate scrumptious feasts at their friends' homes or at the local inns. Poor Cinduri was lucky if she was given a bowl of rice.

*All words appearing in italics in this book are noted and explained in the glossary starting on Page 30.

Working on the farm was
very hard.

—8—

Milking the cows twice a day was no easy chore.

Cinduri could hardly believe
her eyes when she saw
a snake with the jewel
on his head!

One day Cinduri sat down near the lakeshore to rest for a few moments. She was overcome with nostalgic memories of her father and mother. She started to cry. "Why are you crying, Cinduri?" said a voice from the water. Cinduri was frightened for there was nobody there. "Don't be alarmed, Cinduri. I have watched you work yourself to death. I have come to help you. To begin with, I'll take your pot and bring you water that is cool, sweet and *amrit,* fit for gods and kings."

As Cinduri gazed at the ripples of water, she saw the most unusual white water snake with a red jewel on his head. She could hardly believe her eyes. She was hypnotized and passed the pot to the snake who took it and disappeared under the water. Down, down he went and when he reappeared he had Cinduri's pot filled with cool, clear and sweet water, just as he had promised. He also presented her with a gold plate full of delicious *rotis,* succulent vegetables, almond rice and sweetmeats. "Eat this, Cinduri. From now on, you have no need to be hungry again. I have adopted you as a goddaughter, I am your godfather and we are family. As Lord of the Underworld, I can grant you anything you wish." Cinduri folded her hands, thanked Godfather Snake and ate her gift of food. She could not believe her good fortune.

Godfather Snake bestows
magic in Cinduri's life.

When it was time for Cinduri to leave, Godfather Snake said, "Come here whenever you are hungry, unhappy or in need of something special. When you arrive here to summon me, sing the following song:

"Godfather Snake, snake of the magic lake,
Mighty God of the Underworld,
My Godfather, my Shepherd,
Please come to help,
For your daughter's sake."

Cinduri again folded her hands to show reverence as the snake disappeared under water. Every day, the snake provided her with cool, fresh amrit water and a feast. She fed her bowl of rice to the peacocks, green parrots and other birds. Her stepmother could not understand what was happening.

After a few days, it occurred to the stepmother that the quality of the water that Cinduri fetched from the lake had suddenly changed. It was crystal clear, cooler and sweeter than any water she had ever tasted. She also noticed that Cinduri herself was absolutely blooming and more beautiful than ever. The stepmother burned with rage and jealousy and decided to discover the secret of Cinduri's youth and amrit water. She spoke to her daughter, Lata, and asked her to follow Cinduri the next day. Lata secretly followed Cinduri and hid behind a bush. She was absolutely amazed as she watched Godfather Snake come up to meet Cinduri as she sang her song. She watched the snake take the pot and bring back a pot full of amrit water and a plate of delicacies. While Cinduri ate, Godfather Snake commanded the fish, frogs and peacocks to entertain Cinduri with their songs and dancing.

Navaratri
Dance Festival
of Suryanagar.

A little later, after Cinduri returned home, Lata came out of her hiding place and quickly made her way back. She reported to her mother how the strange water snake provided the new magic in Cinduri's life. The stepmother was furious. She was a mean woman who was determined to ruin Cinduri's life and she would not have listened to any warnings from her dreams or even from any fortune tellers. She decided to find a way to foil Cinduri's newfound happiness and fortune.

In the meanwhile, there was an exciting announcement in the town. Two musicians played the drums to gather a crowd, then the messenger announced that the Crown Prince of Suryanagar would visit Cindurnagar on the ninth night of the *Navaratri* festival. It is the time of year twenty days before *Diwali* (Festival of Lights) that precedes the new year's day. For nine evenings, young men and young maidens take the opportunity to assemble under a pavilion to meet friends and perform all the folk dances and also create new dance steps.

How Cinduri longed to go! But her stepmother had different plans. She hoped to find a husband for her own daughter, Lata, and did not want any young men to see the exotic Cinduri who would make a fine impression immediately.

Everybody became excited and started to collect a fabulous selection of the most beautiful golden bodices and skirts to wear with their *saris* and *chundris.* They searched through family heirlooms and treasures to select their golden necklaces, rings, earrings and anklets. "Can I go to the festival with you?" Cinduri timidly asked her stepmother. "What! You go to the Navaratri festival? Who is going to look after our farm, cows and buffaloes? Someone might come and steal our vegetables and animals. Out of the question. You shall stay home and make sure everything is all right." Poor Cinduri was heartbroken.

Aarti homage

On the evening of the ninth Navaratri when the *aarti* is lit, the stepmother and Lata dressed themselves in their finery and drove off to the festival in their smart horse drawn carriage. As soon as Cinduri was alone, she sat down in despair and yearned to go to the festival. She remembered her Godfather Snake and quickly made her way to the lake. When she arrived there, she sang again:

> "Godfather Snake, snake of the magic lake,
> Mighty God of the Underworld,
> My Godfather, my Shepherd,
> Please come to help,
> For your daughter's sake."

The snake came up to greet Cinduri and asked her what she wished for. She explained as she sobbed that she wanted to go to the festival but did not have any clothes or jewellery or a carriage. Godfather Snake soothed her and calmly said, "Now, now, my little pet, you know that I can always help you. Here, take this jewel from my head. Hold it firmly in your hand, rub it and make a wish and it will be granted. Hide the jewel in this silk handkerchief and take good care of it."

Cinduri was transformed
into a beautiful
Princess.

Cinduri did just what she was told to do. Imagine! She was transformed into a beautiful princess wearing magnificent clothes of the finest fabrics and the most precious jewellery of exquisite craftsmanship, studded with rubies. On her ankles were the most precious and beautiful anklets of white gold and diamonds. A horse drawn carriage with a driver and an attendant were ready to drive her to the festival. Just as she was ready to leave, Godfather Snake called out, "Cinduri, go and have a good time but you must return home by midnight, because at that hour the magic will be over." Cinduri thanked Godfather Snake for his jewel, a priceless souvenir all dreams were made of, and promised to come back home at midnight.

When Cinduri arrived at the Navaratri festival, all eyes turned to gaze at her. People whispered all around her, "Look at that beautiful princess! Who can she be?" The Prince of Suryanagar fell in love with her at first sight and asked her for a dance. And would you believe that he danced every dance with Cinduri for the rest of the evening? Cinduri was the life and soul of the festival.

At midnight there was to be an aarti ceremony, A special homage to *Goddess Durga* in whose honour the festival is held every year. The Prince, as the visiting dignitary, was going to perform the aarti and invited Cinduri to join him in the ceremony to receive the goddess's blessings. Cinduri suddenly remembered her promise to Godfather Snake and dashed away, followed by the Prince.

The Prince's eyes caught the sight of
a bright, glittering object on the road.

Cinduri ran like a gazelle and the Prince could not keep up with her. Suddenly, his eyes caught sight of a bright, glittering object on the road. As he bent to pick it up, he realized that it was an anklet from Cinduri's leg. He was fascinated with it and could not forget Cinduri. All he could think of was how to find the girl who had worn that enchanting anklet.

In the meantime, the King of Suryanagar decided that it was time for his son, the Crown Prince, to be married. But when he suggested different princesses and noble ladies to him, the Prince shook his head, "I know who I want to marry," he told his father, "but I don't know how and where to find her." He drew out the enchanting anklet which he had hidden in his robe. "I will marry the owner of this anklet and no one else."

The King sent messengers to every part of his kingdom and proclaimed a grand celebration inviting all the young maidens to come and try on the anklet. The girl whose leg would fit the anklet perfectly would become the Prince's bride.

"Mother, hurry, let's go. I want to wear that anklet. This is my chance to win the Prince," said Lata. "Can I go with you?" asked Cinduri. "Lata and I will go first," the stepmother replied. "You can come later, as soon as you have milked all the cows and buffaloes, fetched the drinking water, and have done your rounds to sell the milk, butter and vegetables."

Cinduri waited for her turn to try on the anklet.

In despair, Cinduri walked out of the house and sat down under a tree. What was the use of hoping for an impossible wish? By the time she would finish her chores, the Prince would have given up and left Cindurnagar. As the tears rolled down her cheeks, she remembered the magic jewel of Godfather Snake. She carefully unrolled the silk handkerchief that she was hiding in her bodice, handled the jewel with tender loving care, rubbed it gently and sang:

> "Jewel, O magic jewel,
> Give a sign or tell,
> Perform my chores and beam me,
> Across to where my beloved awaits me."

In a twinkling of an eye, Cinduri's tasks were done and she was beamed across to the pavilion. In the presence of the Crown Prince, the attendants were busy trying to fit the anklet on the maidens who had assembled there from all over the kingdom. Until Cinduri arrived, all who tried on the anklet found it impossibly small or large. It was Cinduri's turn to try it on. When her stepmother saw Cinduri, she sneered and shouted, "What are you doing here so soon? Have you finished all your chores? I will take the hide off you if you haven't." The Prince ordered her to be quiet and gazed tenderly at Cinduri. "Let her try the anklet," he ordered.

As the servant placed the anklet, Cinduri was transformed into the beautiful Princess with the same attire that she wore the night of the festival.

Cinduri arrived in
a palque (carriage)
supported by two attendants.

From her silk handkerchief, she unwrapped the matching anklet and let the attendant put it on her other leg. The Prince was overjoyed and knew in his heart that he had found his true love. The King was supremely happy that his son had found a bride at last.

A wedding was arranged for the evening of the following full moon. The King ordered the prime minister to make the grand arrangements and plan a great celebration. A gigantic and very artistic wedding invitation was posted at the palace gates. Everyone was invited. Cinduri arrived in a *palque* (carriage) supported by two attendants dressed in their regalia. She looked ravishing and bewitching in her elegant wedding dress. Even the *devas* in the sky were so charmed by her winsome beauty, shy blush and irrepressible gentleness that they sprinkled rice and flowers on her for good luck and fertility.

She walked gracefully in a dignified way to the specially created marquee where a fire was burning for marriage rites. The *conch* was blown. The dashing Prince greeted the captivating young Cinduri with a charming smile. Cinduri and the Prince exchanged *haars* and promised to love and honour each other for the rest of their lives.

Wedding of The Prince
and Cinduri.

The King had a magnificent castle built for his beloved son, the Prince, and Cinduri. Since the stepmother and Lata had been so cruel and unkind to her, the Prince would not permit Cinduri to invite them to live in the castle. They were left to tend their own little farm by themselves and since they did not know the hardships of labour, the farm deteriorated and they went on the road as poor beggars. One day, while they were asleep under a tree, lightning struck and uprooted it and they were crushed to death.

Meanwhile, the Prince and Cinduri enjoyed the luxurious castle built for them and lived happily ever after.

* * * * *

Cinduri
and
The Prince
lived happily
ever after.

—28—

This tale of Cinderella, set in India, is basically the same as the familiar European fairy tale. In India, all literal knowledge was preserved in oral traditions for thousands of years. The Cinderella tale as we know it was preserved as "Nagmani" (Jewel of the Snake). I have adapted it to a modern setting familiar to us. I am inclined to believe that this tale is at least 1,000 years old.

For hunting and gathering societies, the underwater world could be mysterious and threatening, a place ruled by snakes and dragons. If placated with offerings, these creatures rewarded their benefactors by bestowing incredible fortune and good luck. Occasionally, no offering was necessary. The creature simply took pity on an unhappy being and befriended that person.

In many cultures, a snake is a symbol of strength and might. The Egyptian Pharaoh wore a crown with the double headed cobra as a symbol of supreme power. The snake may represent death but its venom is used for medicinal purposes and saves lives. Hence, it is synonymous with wealth, prosperity and royalty.

The snake is revered in some parts of India. Many East Indian and Middle Eastern dances contain movements of a snake that symbolize its importance in that culture. We, in the west, like to wear rings, belts and bracelets with replicas of snakes, so we are not completely free from the enigma and enchantment of this ancient world.

The snake plays a vital role in this story. The magic and reality of the supreme power that is held by the serpent is depicted in order to portray a tale of universal and eternal meaning.

Lila Mehta
Toronto, Ontario, Canada
October 21, 1986

* * * * *

Glossary

aarti
(Pronounced are/tee)

- Both homage performed with a lamp and the lamp itself. Before the clock was invented, people had to rely on shadows cast by the sun, position of the moon in the sky and the performance of the aarti in the temple to tell the time. A midnight aarti was a familiar custom at community gatherings. An aarti is offered to god, goddess, royalty or to an important dignitary.

amrit
(am/rit)

- ambrosia, drink of the gods

chundri
(chun/dree)

- veil worn by a young girl

conch shell blowing

- a large size sea shell which, when blown, creates a reverberating sound. Mainly used at the commencement of a royal marriage ceremony, religious ceremony and major cultural events.

devas
(de/vus)

- angels

Diwali
(di/wu/lee)

- Festival of lights, a unique and the most celebrated autumn (fall) festival of south-east Asia, especially of India.

Goddess Durga
(Door/gah)

- Hindu goddess, destroyer of all evil, also goddess of fertility.

haars (hars)	- garlands of flowers; leis
palque (pul/kee)	- carriage used to carry distinguished individuals. It is generally covered with rich brocades or golden sheets and is carried on the shoulders of individuals of rank or distinction who vied for the honour.
roti (ro/tee)	- a flat wholewheat bread resembling a pancake, main diet of the East Indians.
sari (sah/ree)	- a length of silk or pretty material six yards long, draped around the body over a petticoat. It is worn as a main dress by women of India.
Vikram (Vik/rum)	- a great king of India who lived 2,000 years ago. He was good, just and wise like King Solomon.